WHAT'S WRONG WITH THIS BOOK?

BY

RICHARD McGUIRE

VIKING

VIKING   Published by the Penguin Group
Penguin Books USA Inc., 375 Hudson Street, New York, New York 10014, U.S.A.
Penguin Books Ltd, 27 Wrights Lane, London W8 5TZ, England
Penguin Books Australia Ltd, Ringwood, Victoria, Australia
Penguin Books Canada Ltd, 10 Alcorn Avenue, Toronto, Ontario, Canada M4V 3B2
Penguin Books (N.Z.) Ltd, 182–190 Wairau Road, Auckland 10, New Zealand
Penguin Books Ltd, Registered Offices: Harmondsworth,
Middlesex, England
First published in 1997 by Viking, a division of
Penguin Books USA Inc.

10 9 8 7 6 5 4 3 2 1

LIBRARY OF CONGRESS CATALOGING-IN-PUBLICATION DATA
McGuire, Richard.
What's wrong with this book? / by Richard McGuire.
p.   cm.
Summary : Text and illustrations present such puzzles as a hand that is also the
head of a rabbit and dinosaur shadows that are also clowns with big feet.

WHAT'S WRONG WITH THIS BOOK?

BY RICHARD McGUIRE

VIKING

ISBN 0-670-86852-3 (hardcover)   [1. Picture puzzles. 2. Stories in rhyme.]   I. Title.
PZ8.3.M1595Wh 1997 [E]—dc20   96-36085   CIP AC
Printed in Singapore   Set in Futura
Without limiting the rights under copyright reserved above, no part of this
publication may be reproduced, stored in or introduced into a retrieval
system, or transmitted, in any form or by any means (electronic,
mechanical, photocopying, recording or otherwise),
without the prior written permission of both the
copyright owner and the above
publisher of this book.

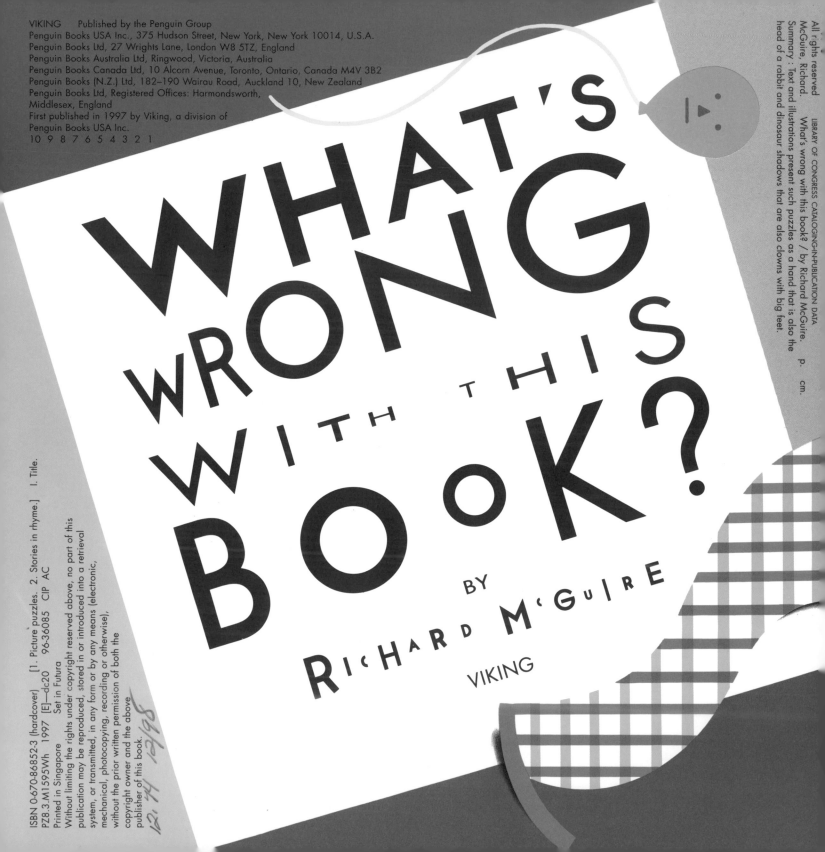

What do you mean, what's wrong with this book?

Nothing is wrong—go on, take a look.

So the story has holes. Well what can I say?

It makes the book better to look through that way.

Don't count the clowns, there are five, I can see.

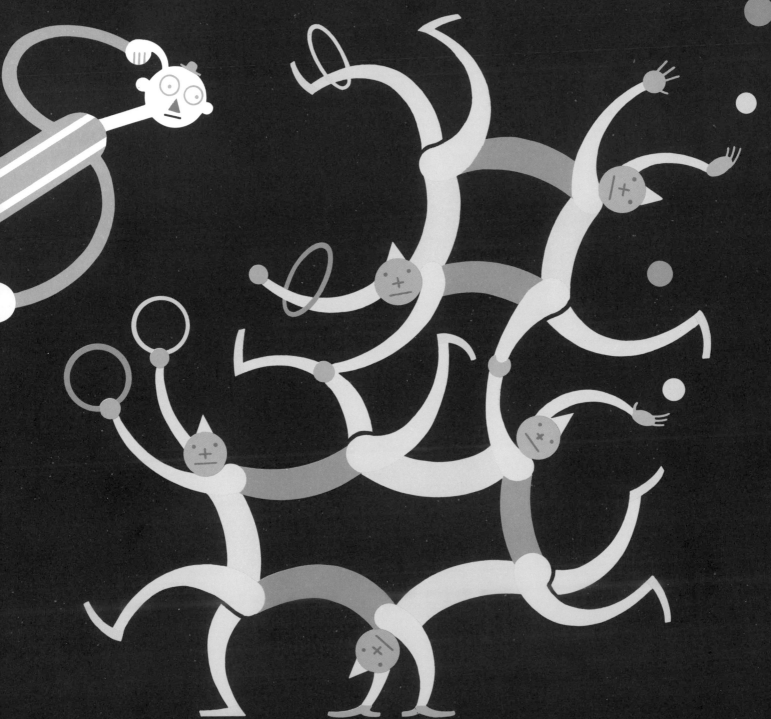

Why bother counting? Don't you believe me?

Why can't a man try to bark for a change?
Dogs understand, so why is it strange?

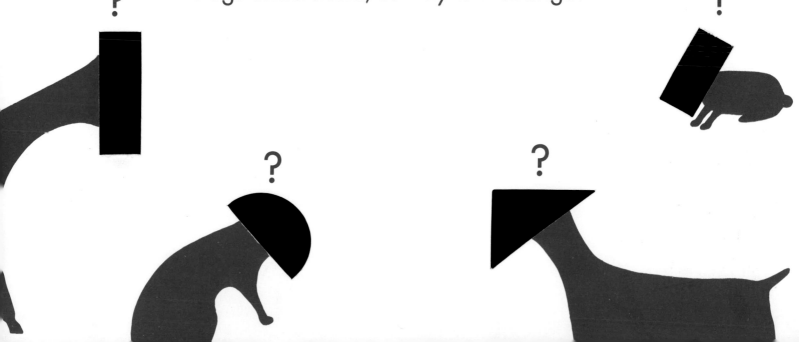

Why can't a hand be the head of a rabbit?
Turn into a dog, a goat, or a parrot?

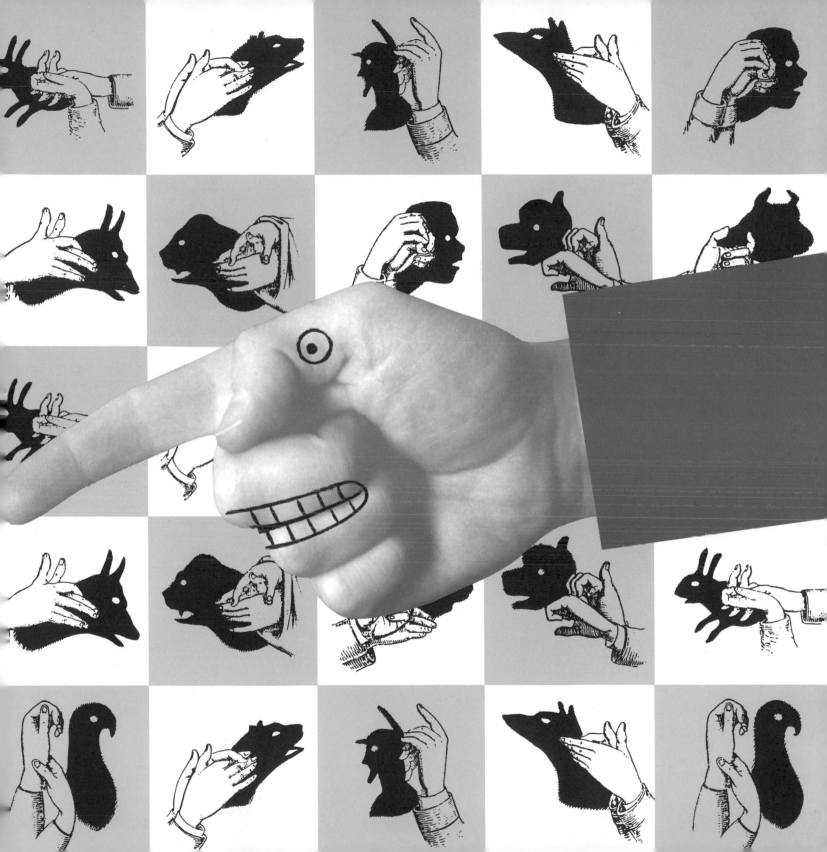

Well, here it's unclear whose shadows are where,
but that doesn't matter. Look over there.

This guy is too wide for his shadow to hide.

You can't see the whole picture from only one side.

I know what this is; what else could it be?
A big jumbo shadow is all that I see.

Well, anyone can make a simple mistake.
Still I wasn't exactly expecting a snake!

Let's go inside

Here's a nice house, you can tell by its face.
How could there be anything wrong with this place?

There's two sides to each story, and both of them true.

Which side is up? I don't have a clue!

Now this is more like it—nice weather too.
Who says there is anything wrong with this view?

Nothing's wrong with the beach—it's perfectly fine.
Does something seem odd? I don't see a sign.

So go right ahead, take a close look.
There is absolutely nothing wrong with this book.

VIKING

RICHARD McGUIRE

BY

BOOK

WITH THIS

WRONG

WHAT'S